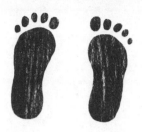

PRAISE FOR THE BIG FOOT AND LITTLE FOOT SERIES

★ "This warmhearted new series, particularly suited for reluctant readers or chapter-book newbies, promises more laughs and exploits from the entertainingly paired Hugo and Boone."
—*Booklist*, starred review

"A charming friendship story." —*Kirkus Reviews*

"Engaging, humorous, and sweet." —*School Library Connection*

BIGFOOT and LITTLE FOOT

BOOK 4

THE BOG BEAST

STORY BY
ELLEN POTTER

ART BY
FELICITA SALA

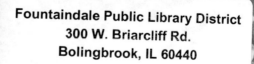

AMULET BOOKS • NEW YORK

The Library of Congress has cataloged the hardcover edition as follows:
Library of Congress Cataloging-in-Publication Data
Names: Potter, Ellen, 1963- author. | Sala, Felicita, illustrator.
Title: The bog beast / story by Ellen Potter ; art by Felicita Sala.
Description: New York : Amulet Books, 2020. | Series: Big Foot and Little Foot book 4 | Audience: Ages 6 to 9. | Summary: On Bimbling Day, when young Sasquatches hope to earn the right to explore the North Woods on their own, Hugo, Boone, and Gigi become stranded and encounter strange and mysterious creatures.
Identifiers: LCCN 2020009344 | ISBN 9781419743221 (hardcover) | ISBN 9781683357919 (ebook)
Subjects: CYAC: Sasquatch–Fiction. | Friendship–Fiction. | Adventure and adventurers–Fiction. | Monsters–Fiction.
Classification: LCC PZ7.P8518 Bog 2020 | DDC [E]–dc23
LC record available at https://lccn.loc.gov/2020009344

Paperback ISBN 978-1-4197-4323-8
Text copyright © 2020 Ellen Potter
Illustrations copyright © 2020 Felicita Sala
Book design by Brenda E. Angelilli

Printed and bound in U.S.A.
10 9 8 7 6 5 4 3 2 1

Amulet Books are available at special discounts when purchased in quantity for premiums and promotions as well as fundraising or educational use. Special editions can also be created to specification. For details, contact specialsales@abramsbooks.com or the address below.

Amulet Books® is a registered trademark of Harry N. Abrams, Inc.

ABRAMS The Art of Books
195 Broadway, New York, NY 10007

The Big Foot and Little Foot series

1

Bimbling Day

Deep in the cold North Woods, there lived a young Sasquatch named Hugo. He was bigger than you but smaller than me, and he was hairier than both of us. He lived in apartment 1G in the very back of Widdershins Cavern with his mother and father and his older sister, Winnie.

Hugo was hopping with excitement that morning because it was Bimbling Day! He brushed his hair very quickly—or as quickly as a Sasquatch can. Remember, Sasquatches have an awful lot of hair to brush. At breakfast, he shoveled down his oatmeal and gooseberries so fast that he choked on it and a gooseberry flew out of his nose.

"Slow down, pal," Hugo's dad said.

But Hugo couldn't slow down. Bimbling Day was a very important day for squidges (a squidge is what you call a young Sasquatch). Bimbling Day was the first day squidges went out into the North Woods all by themselves. The teacher gave each squidge a list of things to collect in the

woods, sort of like a scavenger hunt. If a squidge collected all of those things, they earned a Bimble Badge. That meant they could go into the North Woods on their own whenever they liked. If they didn't collect everything on the list, they had to wait a whole year to try again.

Hugo couldn't wait to bimble (a Sasquatch word for roaming the woods and finding things). He loved the greeny-ness and the sunshiny-ness of the North Woods. But most of all, he loved Ripple Worm River, which twisted and turned through the woods like a giant, glittering worm. The best thing about the river was that his friend Boone lived on the banks of it in a little blue house with a red roof.

When it was time to leave for school, Hugo's mom looked him over carefully. She brushed some stray hairs from his shoulders. Sasquatches shed a lot during the spring.

"You'll be careful today, won't you, Hugo?" Mom said in her worried voice.

"Of course I will," Hugo told her.

"Yeah, you don't want to wind up like Annabelle Loody," his sister, Winnie, said in a spooky voice.

"Who's that?" Hugo asked.

Hugo's mom and dad exchanged a look.

"Don't let her scare you," Dad said to Hugo. He reached out and wiggled Hugo's ear, which is kind of like when a Human tousles another Human's hair. "You'll tell us all about your adventures when you come home."

"*If* you come home," Winnie whispered to him as they left the apartment.

2

The Mystery of Annabelle Loody

Hugo and Winnie started down the dark passageway toward school. The Academy for Curious Squidges & Boone was on the west end of the cavern, and they lived on the east end, so they had a long, winding walk every morning.

"Who's Annabelle Loody?" Hugo asked Winnie.

"Dad said not to scare you, so I'm not telling. See? I'm buttoning my lips." Winnie pretended to button her lips.

"You're just making her up, right?" Hugo said.

But Winnie didn't answer him because her lips were buttoned.

They stopped at apartment 1B. That was where Hugo's friend Gigi lived. Gigi's big sister, Hazel, opened the door, and both she and Gigi joined Hugo and Winnie on their walk to school.

Winnie's lip button must have fallen off, because she started talking to Hazel right away. She squealed when Hazel showed her the latest copy of  *Squoosh*, a magazine for teenage squidges. ("Squoosh" is Sasquatch slang for a cute Sasquatch boy.) Winnie and Hazel immediately starting talking about one of the cute squooshes in the magazine.

"If I ever met him in person," said Hazel, "I would, like, scream and then pass out."

"That would make a good first impression," Gigi said, and rolled her eyes at Hugo. Hugo rolled his eyes back at her. Then he noticed something.

"Hey, what happened to your braid, Gigi?"

"What do you mean?"

"It's not there. You always wear a braid."

"Not today. Braids can get caught in branches. I read about it in this book." Gigi reached into her backpack and pulled out a thick red book. Its title was *Absolutely Everything You Ever Wanted to Know About the North Woods* by Dr. Oliver Feathergill.

"Dr. Feathergill is an explorer. His book gives you all kinds of tips, like what to do in a lightning storm and how to get water from trees. I'm taking the book with me on my bimble."

Hugo was beginning to feel a little worried. "The only things I'm bringing are five acorn butter-and-raspberry cream sandwiches."

"Oh. Well, those are important, too, Hugo," said Gigi brightly. "I just want to be extra prepared for Bimbling Day. After all, none of us wants to wind up like Annabelle Loody."

"Annabelle Loody!? Wait. Is she *real*?" Hugo asked.

"Of course she's real. She's in the book." Gigi patted the big red book. "There's a whole chapter called 'The Mysterious Disappearance of Annabelle Loody.' It says that ten years ago, she went out on Bim-

Ch 6
The Mysterious
Disappearance
of Annabelle Loody

bling Day, and she never returned."

"What happened to her?" Hugo asked.

Gigi shrugged. "No one knows."

"Oh yes they do!" cried Hazel. She and Winnie had stopped looking at *Squoosh* magazine long enough to eavesdrop. "Annabelle Loody was eaten by a Bog Beast."

"Bog Beasts love to eat little squidges," added Winnie, widening her eyes at Hugo and Gigi and smacking her lips. "Yum, yum!"

Gigi just flapped her hand at them. "Don't listen to them, Hugo. They don't know what they're talking about."

"Really?" Winnie replied snarkily. "Hazel and I earned *our* Bimble Badges already, so we know more than you two do."

"Gigi knows everything about everything!" Hugo declared. He meant it, too. Gigi read more books than anyone he knew.

"There's probably a perfectly ordinary reason why Annabelle Loody disappeared," said Gigi.

"Like what?" asked Hugo.

"Well, maybe she got swallowed up by a sinkhole in the bog. Or maybe she fell into the river. Or maybe she got caught by a Human. There are all kinds of things that can go wrong on Bimbling Day."

Bimbling Day had started off seeming so exciting, and now Hugo was beginning to feel more and more nervous. He sighed. Sometimes he wished Gigi didn't know everything about everything.

3

Hair Ball Collection

When Hugo and Gigi arrived at their classroom, Hugo's best friend, Boone, was already there. Boone was carrying a fat backpack. Sticking out of the backpack were a home-made spyglass, a yardstick, and a net on a long pole. On his head was a black wool hat with one long antenna on it.

"Why are you carrying all that stuff?" Hugo asked Boone.

"For Bimbling Day. I always carry my gear when I go walking through the woods. You never know when you might run into a cryptid."

Boone knew all about cryptids, which is a fancy word for mysterious creatures.

"Why are you wearing that hat?" Hugo asked.

Boone reached up to his hat and pulled the antenna down. On its tip was a small round lens. He placed the lens over his eye. "It's a magnifying glass. I'll use it to examine any strange footprints."

"Wow. You thought of everything."

"What did *you* bring?" Boone asked, nodding toward Hugo's backpack.

"Five acorn butter-and–raspberry cream sandwiches," Hugo muttered.

"Oh. That's good, too," said Boone.

"Hey, Boone," Hugo said, trying to keep his voice casual, "have you ever heard of Bog Beasts?"

"Sure. Green, slimy creatures with big claws. They live in swampy areas. The amazing thing about Bog Beasts is that they have plants growing out of their

bodies instead of hair."

"Do you think there are any Bog Beasts around here?" Hugo asked.

Boone thought for a moment. "I wouldn't be surprised. The North Woods are full of strange and mysterious things."

That was true. Once, Hugo and Boone had spotted an Ogopogo, a kind of sea serpent, while they were sailing in Boone's rowboat, the *Voyajer.*

"If we're lucky, maybe we'll see one today," Boone said.

"Yeah, maybe," Hugo agreed uncertainly. "If we're lucky."

"Good morning, class!" Mrs. Nukluk walked in carrying a basket. She swatted at the air as she walked. During shedding season, a classroom full of active squidges can get very hairy. There were strands of squidge hair floating all around, settling in corners, and, worst of all, landing on Mrs. Nukluk's goose-feather cloak. Her cloak had a knack for attracting squidge hair.

Frowning, Mrs. Nukluk picked some hairs off of it.

"Can I have those hairs, Mrs. Nukluk?" Malcolm asked excitedly.

"Why on earth would you want them, Malcolm?"

"For my hair ball collection!" he said. From his backpack, he pulled out a ball of hair the size of a cantaloupe.

Mrs. Nukluk made a face. "Put that thing away, Malcolm." She took a deep breath and turned to the class. "All right, everyone, we will be heading out into the North Woods in just a few minutes. But first"— she reached into her basket and pulled out a red spray can—"I will be giving out cans of Human Repellant."

Mrs. Nukluk gave each squidge and Boone a red spray can. Human Repellant came in handy when you were walking in the woods and suspected there were Humans nearby. When you sprayed it, it smelled just like a skunk. Humans hate that smell. (Sasquatches don't like it very much either, but they don't hate it nearly as much as Humans do.) If a Human smelled it, they would think there was a skunk nearby and leave the area quickly.

Roderick raised his hand. "Mrs. Nukluk, I don't think it's fair that Boone gets to earn a Bimble Badge. He *lives* in the woods. Also, he's a Human. If another Human sees him, it's no big deal!"

"Yes, I've thought about that," Mrs. Nukluk said. "That's why this year you will be going out in teams instead of by yourselves. That will make things fairer."

Everyone clapped at this news! It was much more fun—and much less scary— to explore the North Woods if you had a friend with you.

All the clapping caused a flurry of squidge hair to fly around the classroom.

"Oh my," said Mrs. Nukluk, picking stray hairs off of her goose-feather cloak, "we are shedding a lot, aren't we?"

"More for my hair ball collection!" cried Malcolm as he snatched at the hairs in the air.

4

Teammates

After everyone settled down, Mrs. Nukluk said she would announce the teams.

Hugo and Boone looked at each other and grinned. They knew they made a great team. They had been on adventures together before.

"Boone," Mrs. Nukluk said, "you will team up with Roderick."

Hugo gasped. Boone's eyes widened in shock.

"That's totally unfair!" Roderick cried. "Why do I have to team up with a Human?! He'll just stomp around the woods and blabber loudly. Humans don't know

how to walk quietly in the woods like Sasquatches do."

Mrs. Nukluk gave Roderick a warning look. But she also told Boone he'd have to leave all his noisy cryptid-finding tools in the classroom.

"Pip, Malcolm, and Izzy will be teammates," she continued.

The three of them grinned at one another. Three squidges on a team was even better than two.

"And last but not least . . . Hugo and Gigi will be teammates."

Although Hugo was disappointed not to be paired with Boone, he was glad to be on Gigi's team. She may not have explored the woods already like Boone had,

but she knew everything about everything, and that was almost as good.

"Each team will bring back three items."
Mrs. Nukluk turned and wrote the items
on the blackboard:

1. SOMETHING USEFUL

2. SOMETHING TASTY

3. SOMETHING HEALING

"You must bring back all three items in order to receive your Bimble Badge," said Mrs. Nukluk.

Finally, Mrs. Nukluk had them practice their knoodles, which were the alarm sounds a Sasquatch made when they were in trouble. *Knooodle-knooodle-kooo!* meant that a Human was approaching, while *Knoodle-doodle-kikaroo!* meant that you were hurt, and so on.

Boone had some trouble with the knoodles, since Sasquatches can make some sounds that Humans can't.

Then Mrs. Nukluk went over all the safety rules. When she was finished, she asked, "What should you do if you find yourself in an emergency situation?"

"Don't panic, take a deep breath, then make a plan!" everyone recited back to her.

She smiled. "Okay, class, I think you're ready."

5

Team Captain

When Hugo's class stepped outside Widdershins Cavern and into the North Woods, the first thing they did was roll around in a mud pool. They rolled until all their hair was thick with the goopy mud. After that, they rolled on the ground until leaves and twigs stuck to their muddy hair. They did this to camouflage themselves. If they suddenly smelled a Human nearby, they would drop to the ground and keep very still. With luck, the Human wouldn't notice them.

Boone rolled around in the mud and in the leaves and twigs as well. He didn't really have to, since he didn't need to hide from Humans, but he did it anyway.

When everyone was well camouflaged, Mrs. Nukluk gave each team a different map of the area they needed to explore to find their items.

Boone turned to Hugo. "Good luck, Big Foot," he said.

"Good luck, Little Foot," Hugo said to Boone.

They gave each other a hug. Hugo was careful not to hug too hard, though, since he was much stronger than Boone.

Hugo and Gigi examined their map. It looked like they were going to be bimbling in the southern part of the woods.

"A good team should have a Team Captain," Gigi said.

"But there are only two of us. What if we both vote for ourselves as Team Captain?"

"We don't actually have to vote," Gigi replied. "A Team Captain is the one who naturally takes charge of things."

Gigi took the big red book out of her backpack and flipped through the pages.

"The first thing we'll collect is Bogbean," Gigi said, taking charge. She sounded a lot like a Team Captain. "Bogbean is used to heal aches and pains. That means it counts as our 'something healing.'"

"Bogbean?" Hugo said nervously. "But Bogbean is . . . in the bog."

"Of course, where else would it be? And look." Gigi pointed to the map. "The bog is pretty close by."

"But the Bog Beast lives in the bog!" Hugo blurted out.

"No, it doesn't," said Gigi.

"How do you know it doesn't?"

"Because it's not in the book," she said simply, patting her big red book. "If the Bog Beast were real, Dr. Feathergill would have mentioned it."

They followed the map, walking south. They walked very, very quietly, the way all squidges are taught to walk in the woods. Animals stopped what they were doing to watch them. A rabbit that was nibbling on wildflowers lifted its head and flicked its ears toward them curiously. Two young foxes raced between their legs for a minute before darting away again. (Animals are not

scared of Sasquatches, because they know
a Sasquatch would never hurt them.)

"Almost there," Gigi said, looking at the
map.

Hugo nodded, but he wasn't happy to
hear that. All he could think about was the
Bog Beast and sinkholes and the mystery
of Annabelle Loody.

6

Bogbean

As they got closer to the bog, the trees grew thinner and the grass grew higher. All around them were swampy pools of dark water. A wispy mist swirled close to the ground.

Beneath their feet, the land was getting smooshy. Mrs. Nukluk had taught them to be very careful in bogs. You could step on

something that looked like solid ground
and drop straight into water.

"There it is! Bogbean!" Gigi pointed
to clusters of thin stems with small
white flowers that were growing out of a
pool of swampy water. Bogbean for sure.

Hugo had seen his
grandpa make oint-
ment out of it when
his knees felt achy.

Hugo tried to re-
member everything
Mrs. Nukluk had
taught them about walking through a bog.
But he was so worried about Bog Beasts
that his mind went blank.

"We need to find a long walking stick,"

said Gigi. "That way we can test the water as we walk through it to make sure it's not too deep."

"Right!" said Hugo, thankful that Gigi's brain was working well. He looked around and spotted a long, crooked branch on the ground.

"Got one!" he said, scooping up the branch and handing it to Gigi.

Gigi poked the stick into the pool of water.

"Look, it's not too deep," she said. "The water only covers half the stick."

Slowly and carefully, Hugo and Gigi walked into the murky water. First, Gigi plunged the stick into the water to check the ground ahead of them, and then they took a step forward.

The whole time, Hugo looked around for signs of the Bog Beast. His stomach felt so fluttery that he wouldn't have been able to eat a single acorn butter-and-raspberry cream sandwich. Well, maybe one, but definitely not two.

When they reached the Bogbean, they gathered up some of the plants and carefully put them in their backpacks.

These will make Grandpa's knees feel better, Hugo thought with satisfaction.

From behind the swamp grass across the water Hugo saw something move. He turned in time to see a hand shoot out from behind the grass. It plunged into the water and a moment later pulled out a cluster of plants. There was something strange about the hand. For one thing, it had long claws. And for another, it was covered in green tendrils, as though it had vines growing out of it.

7

Something Tasty

Hugo screamed. It wasn't actually a proper scream. It was more like a very loud squeal.

"What's wrong?" Gigi asked, alarmed.

Hugo looked over at the swamp grass again. The hand was gone. He wondered if it had simply been an otter or a beaver and his imagination had turned it into a Bog Beast.

"I think I stepped on a bee," Hugo lied, then checked the bottom of his foot for a pretend beesting. He didn't want Gigi to think he was acting like a giant chuddle (which is a baby Sasquatch).

While he was checking his foot, Gigi reached into her backpack and pulled out her big red book again. She began flipping through the pages.

"I bet we can find some swamp berries around here for our 'something tasty.' Or we could look for wild mint, but that grows near the river, not in the bog—"

"Wild mint, definitely!" Hugo said. The sooner they left the bog, the better.

As they made their way out of the bog, Hugo kept looking around nervously for anything green and slimy lurking behind the tall grass. Once, out of the corner of his eye, he thought he saw something dart behind a tree. But when he turned around to get a better look, nothing was there.

After a while, the ground beneath Hugo's feet became less smooshy. The trees were taller here and grew closer and closer together. Now they were safely under the canopy of thick woods again, with the sound of Ripple Worm River burbling in their ears and the bog far behind them.

Hugo felt better immediately. He began to think about those five acorn butter-and-raspberry cream sandwiches in his backpack. His stomach growled.

"I think a little snack might be—" he started to say, but Gigi interrupted him.

"Look, Hugo!" Gigi pointed up ahead at a patch of green plants. "Wild mint!"

So they went to work gathering up the mint and carefully wrapping it in a cloth. The fresh minty smell reminded Hugo of his grandfather's mint-and-honey iced tea. Grandpa stored the iced tea in oak barrels to give it a special flavor. Oh, it was delicious with a fat slice of gooseberry pie! Hugo's stomach began to feel growly again.

"Um, Gigi, I was just thinking that now might be the perfect time for a nibble—"

"K'nooba-kaboo!!"

"What was that?" Gigi asked, looking around nervously.

"Probably just a bird," Hugo suggested as he reached into his backpack to feel around for a sandwich. But he stopped when the sound came again, louder this time.

"K'NOOBA-NOOKA-BOOOOOOOOO!!"

"That didn't sound like a bird," Gigi said, her eyes flitting around the woods.

Hugo had to admit that she was right. He began to wonder if Bog Beasts sometimes left the bog.

Hugo and Gigi stood very still, listening carefully. Now the growly feeling in Hugo's stomach was replaced by a nervous fluttery feeling.

The sound came again.

"*K'NUBA-KADEEDLE-OO KA-HOOOOOOOOO!!!*"

"I think it's coming from the river," Gigi whispered.

"*KOOKA-KOO-KAPOOOOKA . . . KOOPOOPLY*—oh, darn it, I can never get my knoodles right . . . *HELP!!!*"

Hugo and Gigi looked at each other in shock.

It was Boone's voice.

8

Big Trouble

They took off running, heading for the sound of Boone's calls for help.

When they reached the river-bank, they looked out at the stretch of water. Hugo had never been to this part of Ripple Worm River before. It curved sharply, like an arm bent at the elbow. The river forked here, and down one of those wide channels, the water grew very rough. It rushed and churned and splashed wildly around large boulders poking out of the river.

"HELP!" came Boone's shout again.

Off in the distance in the channel with the wild water, Hugo spied a tiny island

covered with huckleberry bushes. And in the middle of that island stood Boone, all alone, while the river writhed and thrashed around him.

Hugo jumped up and down and waved until Boone saw him and waved back with both arms.

"Can't he swim to shore?" Gigi asked.

"The water is too rough," Hugo said. "And there are rocks all over."

"I wonder how he wound up there in the first place."

They both watched Boone, trying to figure out a way to help him. Suddenly Hugo turned to Gigi. His eyes were bright with an idea.

"I think I know what to do!" he said.

Hugo led the way as he and Gigi ran as fast as they could, following the riverbank. After a few minutes, they saw it: a small red rowboat lying on its side. Hugo had known exactly where to find the *Voyajer*. Boone always left it in the same spot when he rode his boat to school.

Gigi looked at the *Voyajer* and frowned.

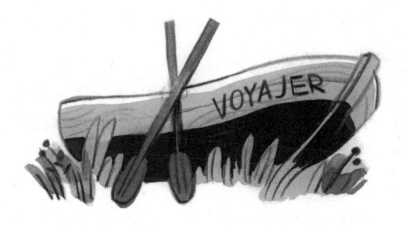

"It seems awfully small," she said in a worried voice.

"It is awfully small," Hugo agreed.

"And that water was running very fast," she said.

"Faster than I've ever seen," said Hugo.

They were silent for a moment. Both of them were thinking about Boone standing alone on the island with the wild water raging around him.

"But you have strong arms for rowing, right?" Gigi said stoutly.

Hugo nodded. "I do. And you are the smartest squidge I know."

"Smart enough," agreed Gigi.

"Okay. Let's go."

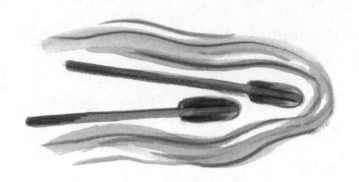

9

The *Voyajer*

In the whole history of Sasquatches, only four Sasquatches had ever been in boats. One of them was Hugo. Another one was a squidge named Nogg. Then there was Dr. Oliver Feathergill. And now there was Gigi.

The water was calm at first. Hugo rowed while Gigi navigated, watching for rocks.

"She's a good boat, isn't she?" said Gigi, patting the *Voyajer*'s side.

"The best," said Hugo.

Ripple Worm River turned sharply. They had reached the fork in the river. Up ahead they could see Boone standing on the little island. The water was churning like a boiling broth.

"Okay, Gigi, here we go!" Hugo said. "Let me know if you see rocks ahead, and I'll steer around them."

"Got it," Gigi said. She sat up straight and squinted at the water ahead of them, looking like a true navigator.

"To your left, Hugo!" she called out.

He saw the rock, a small one, poking out of the water. The current was strong, but so was he, and he steered the *Voyajer* around it.

Hugo smiled. He was feeling pretty confident now.

"Another one off to the right!" Gigi called. After he steered past that, she cried out, "A big one after that, Hugo, to the left, TO THE LEFT!"

There were more and more rocks now. The strange thing was that they seemed to pop up out of nowhere. One minute there was a stretch of unbroken water, and suddenly they'd spot a rock they hadn't noticed before. And even worse, the current was getting stronger and stronger. Hugo was having a hard time controlling the oars as the *Voyajer* tipped this way and that.

Up ahead, Boone was watching them anxiously. He knew how dangerous the river was here.

"Hugo, there are two huge rocks dead ahead!" Gigi cried.

Hugo saw them—two boulders that had suddenly appeared right in their path. He tried to steer the *Voyajer* around them, but Ripple Worm River had other ideas. The powerful current swooped them straight toward the boulders, and a second later, the *Voyajer* was hopelessly wedged between the two big rocks.

The racing water splashed and sprayed and churned all around them.

"We're stuck, Gigi!" Hugo yelled over the water's roar.

"See if you can push us off the rocks with your oars!" Gigi yelled back.

Hugo lifted his right oar out of the water, jammed it up against one of the rocks, and gave a mighty push.

That was when both rocks suddenly sank down into the water and disappeared.

Hugo and Gigi looked at each other. They were too surprised to speak.

Hugo remembered what Boone had

said about the North Woods being full of strange and mysterious things. Vanishing rocks must be one of them.

The very next moment, the current made the *Voyajer* tilt sharply to one side.

Hugo and Gigi screamed but managed to stay inside the boat. The oars, however, did not. They flew right out of Hugo's hands, and the river carried them away.

With no oars, Hugo could not control the *Voyajer* at all. And the thing that worries me (and will probably worry you, too) is that Sasquatches can't swim.

There was nothing for Hugo and Gigi to do but hold on tight and let the wild river take them where it liked. They could see Boone just ahead, pacing the island, calling directions that they couldn't hear over the sound of the river.

They both saw the wave at the same time. It was large and wide and aiming straight for them.

"Hugo!" Gigi shouted, panicked.

"I see it!"

Without oars, there was nothing they could do. The wave crashed against the boat, and the *Voyajer* and Hugo and Gigi were flung upward.

When they came back down, they were on land. And Boone, with all of his thirty-eight freckles, was grinning at them.

10

Prank

You did it!" Boone cried.

"*We* did it," Gigi agreed with happy astonishment.

But once they looked around for the *Voyajer,* their happiness turned to dismay. The poor boat was lying on the island with its hull bashed in.

"Oh, Boone, I'm so sorry," Hugo said.

He felt an ache in the pit of his stomach. The *Voyajer* was like a friend to them. She had taken Hugo and Boone on their best adventures—finding an Ogopogo, sailing to the haunted Craggy Cavern.

Boone walked up to his beloved boat and knelt beside her. He ran his hands over her injured hull.

"Can you fix her?" Hugo asked.

Boone hesitated. "Maybe," he said, but Hugo thought he didn't sound very hopeful.

"How did you wind up here, anyway?" Gigi asked Boone.

"It was all Roderick's idea," said Boone as he plopped himself down beside the *Voyajer* glumly. "The whole time we were bimbling, Roderick wouldn't even talk to me. Then he got really annoyed because I was the one who found our 'something healing' and our 'something useful.' All we needed was our 'something tasty.' That's when I spotted the huckleberry bushes on this island."

The mention of huckleberries

reminded Hugo of the five acorn butter-and-raspberry cream sandwiches in his backpack. His stomach rumbled. But he told himself that this probably wasn't the right time for a snack.

"There was a big tree on the riverbank that had fallen over," Boone continued. "It was so long that it reached across the water and onto the island like a bridge. Roderick said that if I crossed it, he would hold it steady for me. So I did. I collected loads of huckleberries. But when I was ready to go back to shore, Roderick gave the tree a shove, and it floated away. He just stood there and laughed at me like it was a great prank. But then he must have spotted something in the woods that scared him,

because suddenly he screamed and ran away. I haven't seen him since."

"Maybe something happened to him," said Gigi ominously.

"Maybe he ran into a Human," Hugo suggested.

"Or maybe he ran into a Bog Beast," said Gigi in a strange voice.

"But you said Dr. Feathergill never mentioned Bog Beasts in his book," said Hugo.

"Maybe Dr. Feathergill doesn't know everything," Gigi replied, squinting at the water and frowning.

Hugo and Boone looked, too. Something was floating in the river. Something big and green and slimy. At first Hugo thought it was a large clump of weeds. But then he saw a pair of clawed hands paddling at the water.

The Bog Beast was headed right for them.

11

The Bog Beast

They watched the creature swim closer and closer, skillfully weaving its way through the current.

"What do we do, Gigi?" Hugo said.

"I don't know."

Those were words Hugo had hardly ever heard come out of Gigi's mouth. And this was the very worst time to hear them.

Hugo remembered what Mrs. Nukluk had told them to do in an emergency.

Don't panic, take a deep breath, then make a plan.

So that's what Hugo did. He took a deep breath. Then he thought. And finally, he came up with a plan.

"Everyone, grab your Human Repellant!" Hugo said. His voice was very sure and loud. It sounded like someone who was taking charge.

In fact, it sounded very much like a Team Captain.

"Do you think Human Repellant will work on a Bog Beast?" Gigi asked as she took out her spray can.

"Of course. Skunks smell bad to everyone, and we'll be spraying three cans at the same time," said Hugo confidently as he took his spray out of his backpack. "Get ready, everyone!"

They all held up their cans. The Bog Beast was so close now that they could see the green tendrils of its body rippling in the water as it swam.

"Get set!" Hugo yelled. They put their fingers on the spray buttons. The Bog Beast reached up out of the water, its clawed hand grabbing the bottom of a huckleberry bush.

Now they could see the beast clearly. It had green twists of weedy hair that hung over its forehead and coiled around its head, then draped all the way down its thick body, dripping with river water.

"Should we spray now, Hugo?" Boone asked.

"Oooh, I wish you wouldn't," the Bog Beast said in a fast, breathless voice. "Human Repellent makes my eyes swell up."

It's a very shocking thing for a monster

to talk to you. Hugo was so surprised that he forgot to yell "SPRAY!"

"How does it know this is Human Repellant spray?" Gigi wondered out loud.

That's a good question, thought Hugo. He wished he had asked it, especially if he wanted to keep being Team Captain.

"It says so right on the cans," the Bog Beast replied.

Which was very true.

"But how do you know it makes your eyes swell up?" asked Boone.

Another excellent question! thought Hugo. As Team Captain, he should probably think of something clever to say, too.

And suddenly he did.

"I know how," Hugo announced.

Gigi and Boone looked at him with interest, which made Hugo feel more like Team Captain again.

Hugo turned to the beast and glared at it. "You know about Human Repellant because Annabelle Loody sprayed you with it, didn't she? Right before you ate her."

"Ate her? Ooooh, no, no, no," the Bog Beast said in its peculiar breathless way. "That's not true, not true at all."

"I don't believe you," Hugo said, raising

his can of Human Repellent and aiming it at the beast.

"Don't spray!" Gigi cried, jumping between him and the Bog Beast. "The Bog Beast *didn't* eat Annabelle Loody. The Bog Beast *is* Annabelle Loody."

12

Sticky Grass

Hugo and Boone looked from the Bog Beast to Gigi and back again. That made no sense. The Bog Beast was green and slimy and had claws.

"Um, Gigi," Boone said quietly, "I think you may be wrong about this one."

"I'm not. Look." Gigi pointed at the Bog

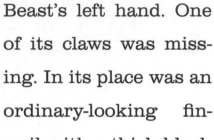

Beast's left hand. One of its claws was missing. In its place was an ordinary-looking fingernail with a thick black splotch on it.

"That black stuff is pine sap glue," said Gigi. "You use it to glue on fake fingernails. Or claws, in this case."

"Are you sure?" Hugo asked.

"Of course I'm sure. I read it in . . ." Gigi muttered something.

"What did you say?" Hugo asked.

Gigi looked at him squarely and said, "I read it in *Squoosh* magazine."

"You read *Squoosh* magazine?" Hugo asked, stunned.

"I read *everything*, Hugo," Gigi replied firmly.

Gigi suddenly reached out, and with a yank, she pulled two handfuls of green, weedy hair from the beast's arm. Everyone gasped, including the Bog Beast. Then, to everyone's shock, Gigi put some of it in her mouth and chewed. After a moment, she spat it out and announced, "Sticky Grass. That's what I thought."

"Does it taste good?" Hugo couldn't help but ask. It had been a long time since he'd had breakfast.

"It tastes like

spinach and vinegar," she said, which didn't sound very appetizing. "Sticky Grass has little burs on it that make it sticky. Watch." She pressed some of the grass onto her own arm, and it stuck.

They all looked at the Bog Beast. In the spot where Gigi had pulled off the Sticky Grass, there was thick, reddish-brown hair. Sasquatch hair.

They had found Annabelle Loody.

13

Annabelle Loody

I remember how excited I was about Bimbling Day—ooooh yes, so excited!" Annabelle told them when they asked what had happened to her all those years ago. "A whole day outside the cavern, all by myself! And such a beautiful day! The sun was peeping though the trees, and the birds were busy with their nests. Every so often, I stopped to watch the honeybees or to pet a deer." Annabelle's voice was dreamy with the memory. "I bimbled and bimbled, and before I knew it, I was completely lost. But I didn't mind—no, no, not at all. Back in the cavern, I lived with my aunt, who didn't like me very much. She said I was an odd bird. Loony Loody, she called me. I didn't fit in at school, either. But the woods! Oh, the woods were wonderful! That night, I slept in the high grass near the bog with the stars watching over me. When I woke up, I was covered with Sticky Grass. 'Well, I look just like a monster, don't I!' I thought. That's when I realized it was a perfect disguise. So, poof! Annabelle Loody disappeared"—she made

a wavy gesture with her hands—"and the legend of the North Woods Bog Beast began."

"But wait . . . you can swim," Hugo said. "You're a Sasquatch, and you can swim."

"Of course I can," Annabelle said. "So can you. It's just that most Sasquatches never bother to learn."

This was big news for Hugo! He had always wished he could swim.

"Once I get my Bimble Badge," Hugo declared, "I'm going to learn how."

"I'll teach you," offered Boone.

"And how are we going to get our Bimble Badges if we can't even get off this island?" Gigi reminded them sensibly as she tucked the Sticky Grass she'd pulled from Annabelle's arm into her backpack.

At that moment, Annabelle Loody lifted her chin and began to howl.

Hugo, Gigi, and Boone all exchanged looks, as if to say, *We like Annabelle, we really do, but she may be a little odd.*

Suddenly, little circles began to form in the river, like water circling a drain. Then . . .

SPLOOSH!

A huge head rose out of the water. It looked like a horse's head, only much larger and with a pair of horns. Its neck was long and thick and snaky. Its skin was silver and smooth, glistening with river water.

"What *is* that?" Gigi asked.

"Is that a—?" Hugo started to say, but Boone interrupted him with a whoop of joy.

"It's an Ogopogo!"

14

Ripple Worms

Actually, they're called Ripple Worms," Annabelle corrected.

"I read about Ripple Worms in Dr. Feathergill's book!" Gigi said. "There are lots of old legends about them. Ripple Worm River is named after them."

Boone looked at the creature thoughtfully. "I think an Ogopogo and a Ripple

Worm are the same thing. They're both river monsters. People just gave them different names."

The Ripple Worm looked at them with large dark eyes. Then it tossed up its head and snorted a spray of water out of its nose slits.

Annabelle howled again.

Another little circle began to form in the

water, and then—*SPLOOSH!*—a new Ripple Worm popped out of the river. This one was smaller, a darker silver, with white speckles on its skin.

SPLOOSH!

SPLOOSH!

SPLOOSH!

More and more Ripple Worms appeared all around the island. Some were

bluish gray, some were silver, and some were black as onyx. Their necks were so long that their heads towered over Hugo, Boone, and Gigi, looking down at them with calm, dark eyes as big as bowling balls. Their long, snaky bodies coiled and uncoiled in the water, each coil rising up like a rock in the river.

It was then that Hugo realized the appearing and disappearing rocks had not been rocks at all. They had been Ripple Worms' coils, rising up and sinking down in the water.

"This is their favorite spot in the river," Annabelle explained. "The rushing water tickles their skin." She giggled and made tickling motions in the air with her claws.

"They don't bite, do they?" Gigi asked nervously.

"Of course not!" said Annabelle indignantly.

Hugo and Gigi were not convinced, though. It was Boone who found the courage to walk to the edge of the island, near a dusky-blue Ripple Worm. He stretched his hand up to pet the creature's head. The Ripple Worm pulled its head back at first. But when Boone kept his hand there, the Ripple Worm lowered its head and let Boone pet its snout.

"Its nose is sooo soft," Boone said dreamily.

Feeling braver, Hugo went up to a sleek black Ripple Worm bobbing in the waves. It

swiveled its head around, watching Hugo cautiously.

"Hi there, fellow," he whispered.

"She's *not* a fellow!" said Annabelle, aghast.

"Oops, sorry about that," Hugo told the Ripple Worm. He reached out and petted her nose. It had a rubbery feel to it. He tickled her, and she made a happy humming sound.

Gigi kept her distance from the creatures, her hands behind her back. But Annabelle wrapped a green arm around Gigi and led her to a very small and beautiful pale silver Ripple Worm.

"He's just a baby," Annabelle told her.

Of course, Gigi felt it would be ridiculous

to be afraid of a baby. She scratched the little Ripple Worm behind his stubby horn. He nuzzled her neck, nibbling at her hair.

After a moment, Annabelle said, "Okay, everyone choose one."

"What do you mean?" Hugo asked her.

"Choose a Ripple Worm to take you back to shore," Annabelle said.

"Wait. Does she want us to ride these things?" Hugo whispered to Boone.

"I think so!" cried Boone happily. He patted the dusky-blue Ripple Worm. "I choose this guy!"

Hugo looked around at all the Ripple Worms. To be honest, he wasn't too thrilled with the idea of riding one—their bodies looked pretty slippery—but he chose the black one since she seemed to like him.

Gigi chose the small silver one. Even though he was a baby, he was an awfully *big* baby.

Annabelle helped Hugo onto his Ripple Worm first.

"They have rows of fins on their bellies," Annabelle instructed Hugo. "You can hook your feet behind her fins to keep from slipping off. Then wrap your arms around her neck."

Hugo scooched up the Ripple Worm's body until his feet met a pair of large, paddle-shaped fins. He wedged his feet behind them and wrapped his arms around the Ripple Worm's neck.

Next Annabelle helped Gigi onto the
silver baby Ripple Worm. He was squirmy
at first, and he coiled up his back, lifting

Gigi high in the air. She screeched and flattened herself against the creature, clutching him so she wouldn't fall off. But after that he settled down.

"Wait! What about the *Voyajer*?" said Boone before he hopped onto his Ripple Worm. "I can't just leave her here."

"The *Voyajer*?" Annabelle looked around the island in case there was someone else she hadn't noticed.

"My boat." Boone pointed to the poor bashed-in boat.

"Oh! That's easy. I can tow her," Annabelle said.

She tied the *Voyajer*'s tow rope to the tail of a dark gray Ripple Worm whose horns were so large that they curled back on themselves, and then she leapt onto its back. With a quick pat on its side, Anna-belle whooped a high-pitched cry, and the next moment all the Ripple Worms dove into the wild river.

15

SPLASH!

Hugo hugged the Ripple Worm's neck tightly as she wound this way and that, slicing through the water. When Hugo began to slip sideways off the Ripple Worm's back, she coiled up her spine to shift Hugo upright again. Sometimes the Ripple Worm leapt out of the water and plunged back down—

SPLASH!—making Hugo laugh and brace his legs against the creature. The wind whipped his hair around, and the water sprayed his face, and all in all it was the most thrilling thing he had ever done in his whole entire life.

Up ahead, he saw Boone on the dusky-

blue Ripple Worm, his arms raised in the air like a daredevil. Hugo turned around and waved to Gigi on the pale silver Ripple Worm. She let go long enough to wave back and flashed a wide smile.

The ride was over too quickly. The Ripple Worms slowed down when they neared the riverbank, then bobbed in the shallow water as Hugo, Boone, and Gigi hopped off and waded to shore. Annabelle untied the *Voyajer* and dragged it onto the shore, too.

"That was so much fun!" Boone said to Annabelle, grinning.

"The Ripple Worms like you," Annabelle said approvingly to them. "If you visit me sometime, you can ride them again." Suddenly, her expression turned serious, and she added, "You won't tell anyone you met me, right?"

"Of course not!" they all assured her.

"The mysterious disappearance of Annabelle Loody will *stay* a mystery," Gigi said. "But Annabelle, don't you miss being home?"

"I *am* home!" replied Annabelle, surprised at the question. "And I know we may not look alike"—she gestured toward the Ripple Worms in the water—"but if friends were berries, I'd pick them every time."

"I know what you mean," said Boone, whose own friends were covered with hair and had feet the size of snow shovels.

"There is one thing I do miss," Annabelle said hesitantly. "It's sort of silly."

"What is it?" asked Gigi.

"Well . . . I really miss . . ." She bit her lip and seemed to consider whether she should tell them or not.

"You can say it," urged Boone.

"Okay. Well . . . I really miss acorn butter sandwiches!" she blurted.

So of course Hugo knew exactly what to do. His belly let out a little growl of disapproval, but he ignored it. He reached into his backpack, and he handed Annabelle his acorn butter-and-raspberry cream sandwiches—all five of them.

She squealed with delight and immediately bit into one of them.

"Oh, and by the way," she said with her mouth full, "there's a squidge hiding in a log just up the hill. He stuffed himself in there when he saw me a while ago. You should probably tell him that it's safe to come out."

16

Roderick

They found Roderick squeezed inside a hollow log. In fact, he had wedged himself in there so tightly that he was good and stuck.

"I think we should leave him there awhile longer," said Hugo to Boone quietly. "Just to teach him a lesson for what he did to you."

"Nah. If it weren't for him, we'd never have met Annabelle and the Ripple Worms. And just think—now we have a new chapter for our book!"

Boone and Hugo planned to write a book called *The Adventures of Big Foot and Little Foot.* It would be about their adventures as cryptozoologists (which is just a fancy word for people who study cryptids).

Gigi was looking at her big red book to figure out how to get a squidge out of a hollow log. Amazingly, Dr. Feathergill had a solution for it. They scraped the moss off the log and packed it all around Roderick. That made him slippery enough to be yanked out with a few hard tugs on his arms.

Roderick didn't even say "Thank you" or "I'm sorry" or "I'll never be mean to Boone again." Instead, he looked all around the woods, his eyes wide with dread.

"Where is it? *Where is it?!*" he shouted in a panicked voice.

"Where is what?" Boone asked.

"The Bog Beast!" Roderick bellowed. "It was green and slimy, and it had claws . . ."

"Don't be ridiculous, Roderick," Gigi said. "There's no such thing as a Bog Beast."

"But I saw it!" He marched around the area, looking behind trees and under bushes.

"You are doing a lot of stomping," said Boone.

"And a lot of loud blabbering," said Hugo.

"Kind of like a Human," said Boone.

That quieted Roderick right down.

The day had been so eventful that it wasn't until they were all back at Widdershins Cavern that Hugo realized something terrible.

"Oh no!" he cried.

"What is it?" Gigi asked.

"We forgot to get our 'something useful.' We won't get our Bimble Badges without it! We'll have to wait a whole year for the next Bimbling Day."

"But we did get our 'something useful,'" she assured him.

And when she told him what it was, he shook his head in wonder.

"You really are the smartest squidge I know, Gigi," he said.

Gigi smiled. "Smart enough."

17

The Bimble Badge Ceremony

The Bimble Badge Ceremony was held a few days later in Mrs. Nukluk's classroom. It was in the evening so that all the squidges' families and friends could attend. Even Boone's grandma came to the ceremony, wearing her fanciest hat with purple feathers.

There were lots of refreshments, which

were made from the things the class had collected on their bimbles. Hugo's grandfather brought a barrel of mint-and-honey iced tea made from the mint leaves that Hugo and Gigi had found. Pip's mother brought soup that she'd made from the wild asparagus Pip's team had brought back. Best of all, Boone's grandmother had made huckleberry cobbler. All the Sasquatches said it was the best huckleberry cobbler they'd ever tasted. Well, everyone except for Mrs. Rattlebags, Roderick's mother. She said she'd had better. But that's just how she was.

One by one, each team went up to Mrs. Nukluk's desk to receive their badges. They were handsome badges carved from

wood with tiny woodland animals and plants etched into them. On the tops were the words OFFICIAL BIMBLE BADGE.

After Hugo and Gigi received their badges and everyone clapped—Hugo even heard Winnie yell, "Nice going, Hugo!"—Mrs. Nukluk said, "I owe Hugo and Gigi special thanks for something they gave me."

She opened her desk drawer, pulled out a pair of gloves, and put them on. They were not pretty gloves. In fact, they were very odd looking. They were completely covered with grass.

"These are grooming gloves. Hugo and Gigi made them out of Sticky Grass as their 'something useful.'" With her gloved hands, she swiped at her goose-feather cloak, then held up the gloves for every-

one to see. The shed squidge hair had stuck to the gloves. Now she could keep her cloak free of hair!

"Can I have that hair, Mrs. Nukluk?" Malcolm called out.

Mrs. Nukluk was in such a good mood that she plucked the squidge hair off the glove and gave it to him. He promptly added it to his hair ball.

"We have one more special surprise," said Mrs. Nukluk. "Please follow me."

They all followed Mrs. Nukluk through

the cavern's winding passageways and out into the North Woods. It was a beautiful warm evening with a starry sky peering through the trees. The chirps of crickets and the *weep-weep*s of tree frogs filled the air. Mrs. Nukluk sniffed in all directions to make sure there were no Humans nearby. Then she led the group down past the five hemlock trees to the glittering waters of Ripple Worm River.

There, waiting on the riverbank, was the *Voyajer.* The little rowboat had been beautifully repaired and had even been given a fresh coat of paint, which gleamed in the moonlight. Two brand-new oars were lying on her seat.

Boone yelped with joy at the sight of her.

"Hugo's grandfather repaired her," Mrs. Nukluk explained.

Even Hugo was surprised. "How do you know how to fix boats, Grandpa?"

"Sasquatches may not sail in boats," Grandpa said, "but repairing one is not much different from repairing the wooden barrels I use for my iced tea. They both need to be leakproof."

"Sasquatches *should* sail in boats!" Boone said. "You see all kinds of amazing things when you travel on the water!"

Hugo and Gigi smiled at each other,

both thinking about Annabelle Loody and their rides on the Ripple Worms.

"Come on!" Boone urged. "I'll take you all for rides in the *Voyajer*. Who wants to go first?"

No one said anything for a moment. The Sasquatches looked around at one another nervously.

"Boats are for Humans," declared Mrs. Rattlebags proudly. "Sasquatches don't like them."

But then Hugo's grandpa stepped forward.

"I'll go," he volunteered.

Boone helped Grandpa into the boat. He rowed the *Voyajer* up the river a little and let Grandpa row it back.

"It *is* fun! Oh, it really is!" Grandpa called from the boat as he rowed.

Mrs. Nukluk went next, and after that, all the Sasquatches wanted rides. Well, all of them except Mrs. Rattlebags and Roderick, but that's just the way they were.

The Sasquatches took turns riding up and down the river until late into the night. Some asked to ride a second time, then a third, and Boone was happy to oblige.

If a Human had stepped outside of their house in the North Woods that night, they would have heard strange *woop-woop*s and *hooroo-hooroo*s, and they would have wondered what they were.

But you and I know.

We know it was the sound of happy

Sasquatches who had just discovered something important: that Sasquatches like riding in boats just as much as Humans do.

Maybe even more.

Woop-woop! Hooroo-hooroo!

ACKNOWLEDGMENTS

Sasquatches know that we all need help if we want to do things right, and that's why I want to thank my wonderful "Sasquatch Community." Major thanks to my editor, Erica Finkel, for her clear-sighted wisdom. I am forever grateful to my agent, Alice Tasman, who is even better than thirty jars of acorn butter. Thanks to Felicita Sala for bringing Hugo and his friends to life with her beautiful illustrations. Big thanks to my publicist, Kimberley Moran, and the entire Abrams team for spreading the word about Hugo and Boone. And finally, as always, thanks to my practically perfect husband, Adam, and my own squidge, Ian.

**THE ADVENTURES OF BIG FOOT AND
LITTLE FOOT CONTINUE IN
BOOK FIVE:**

THE GREMLIN'S SHOES

TURN THE PAGE FOR A SNEAK PEEK!

1

Nothing-to-do-itis

Deep in the cold North Woods, there lived a young Sasquatch named Hugo. He was bigger than you but smaller than me, and he was hairier than both of us. He lived in apartment 1G in the very back of Widdershins Cavern with his mother and father and his older sister, Winnie.

It was Saturday, so there was no school. Hugo and his best friend, Boone, sat on the floor of Hugo's bedroom, dipping their fingers into the little stream that ran through the room. Tiny silver fish swam in the stream. Boone and Hugo made their hands into tunnels for the fish to swim through.

"So, what do you want to do today?" Boone asked Hugo for the fifth time that morning.

"I don't know. What do you want to do today?" Hugo replied, also for the fifth time.

"I don't know," said Boone.

Hugo and Boone had a bad case of Nothing-to-do-itis. You've probably had

Nothing-to-do-itis once or twice in your life, too. It's when you suddenly have loads of free time, but you can't think of a single thing to do with it.

"Are those new shoes?" Hugo asked Boone.

Boone nodded and looked proudly at his red sneakers with black stripes and yellow laces. "The old ones were getting too small."

Hugo didn't have to wear shoes. Sasquatches have tough padding on the soles of their feet so they can walk barefoot. Still, Hugo thought it might be fun to wear red sneakers with black stripes and yellow laces.

Right then, he made a mental list of Reasons Why It Would Be Fun to Be a Human. "Sneakers" was number one on the list.

"Grandma told me that if my feet keep growing so fast," Boone said, "they'll be as big as a Sasquatch's in no time."

He placed his foot next to Hugo's foot to compare. Boone's foot was only half as big as Hugo's. But because Hugo didn't want to discourage Boone, he replied, "Bigger, maybe."

They were quiet for a moment. Then Boone asked for the sixth time, "So, what do you want to do today?"

Hugo was about to reply "I don't know" again when suddenly, he did have an idea.

"We could go to Uncle Figgy's Toy Store," he suggested.

"Yes! That's exactly what we should do!" Boone said, jumping to his feet.

And just like that, their case of Nothing-to-do-itis was cured.

ELLEN POTTER is the award-winning author of many books for children, including the Olivia Kidney series, *Slob*, *The Kneebone Boy*, and most recently, the Piper Green and the Fairy Tree series. She lives in upstate New York.

FELICITA SALA is an award-winning illustrator of the Big Foot and Little Foot series, *The Hideout*, *Be a Tree*, and more. She has worked on several animation projects, but her passion is making picture books. She lives in Rome with her family.

READ THESE OTHER GREAT CHAPTER BOOKS!